The Letter on Light Blue Stationery

A STORY ABOUT BEING SPECIAL

Written by
JOY BERRY

WORD INC.
Waco, Texas 76796

About the Author and Publisher

Joy Berry's mission in life is to help families cope with everyday problems and to help children become competent, responsible, happy individuals. To achieve her goal, she has written over two hundred self-help books for children from birth through age twelve. Her work revolutionized children's publishing by providing families with practical, how-to, living skills information that was previously unavailable in children's books.

Joy gathered a dedicated team of experts, including psychologists, educators, child developmentalists, writers, designers, and artists, to form her publishing company and to help produce her work.

The company, Living Skills Press, produces thoroughly researched books and audio-visual materials that successfully combine humor and education to teach subjects ranging from how to clean a bedroom to how to resolve problems and get along with other people.

Copyright © 1987 by Joy Berry
Living Skills Press, Sebastopol, CA
All rights reserved.
Printed in the United States of America.

Managing Editor: Ellen Klarberg
Copy Editor: Kate Dickey
Contributing Editors: Marilyn Berry, Libby Byers,
Donna Fisher, Michael McBride, Gretchen Savidge
Editorial Assistant: Sandy Passarino

Art Director: Laurie Westdahl
Design: Laurie Westdahl
Production: Caroline Rennard
Illustration design: Bartholomew
Inker: Berenice Happé Iriks
Colorer: Berenice Happé Iriks
Composition: Dwan Typography

Published by Word Incorporated in cooperation with Living Skills Press.

Hello, my name is Joy, and I'd like to tell you a story about Pamela and an important lesson she learned about the value of each and every person.

In her whole life Pamela had never known a person who had died. A goldfish she won at the school carnival died, and her very first cat was killed when it was hit by a car.

Pamela felt bad when her fish and cat died, but they were pets, not people. Pamela would soon learn that the death of a pet is different from the death of a person.

It all began one day when Pamela came home from school. "I'm home!" Pamela announced, as she walked into the house and closed the door behind her.

Her mother responded to Pamela's proclamation by calling out from the family room, "Pamela, please come here. I need to talk to you."

"Oh oh, something must be wrong," Pamela muttered to herself.

She walked into the family room and found her mother sitting at the table, writing a note on some light blue stationery.

The look on her mother's face confirmed Pamela's suspicions. She wasn't looking forward to hearing what her mother had to say.

Pamela placed her school books and lunch box on the table and heaved a big sigh as she settled into a chair.

Solemnly, her mother began to speak. "Mrs. McAlister called today. She told me that Audrey Steinhoffer had gone to her aunt's house to spend the weekend. Audrey and her aunt were driving to the grocery store when another car crossed over the center line and hit them head on. Audrey's aunt was hurt very badly and . . ." Pamela's mother paused, took a deep breath and then went on, ". . . Audrey was killed."

Pamela jumped to her feet. "Killed? Audrey Steinhoffer killed?" She gasped in disbelief.

"Yes, sweetheart, Audrey Steinhoffer is dead," Pamela's mother affirmed softly.

Pamela began pacing back and forth, nervously wringing her hands as she walked.

It was unlike Pamela to talk before she thought about every word she was going to say. But at the moment, her brain was too stunned to think. So, unconsciously, she began to ramble on and on. "It can't be true. It's impossible. I just saw Audrey on Friday. We were at the same lunch table together. I've been going to school with Audrey since kindergarten. I don't believe it. No . . ."

Realizing that the news of Audrey's death affected Pamela deeply, Pamela's mother stood up and walked over to her distraught daughter. Lovingly she put her arms around Pamela and tried to console her. Then she carefully continued the conversation. "I'm writing Audrey's parents a sympathy letter, and I think it would be nice if you would write one too."

"But . . . but what would I say?" Pamela stammered.

Her mother thought for a moment and then responded, "Why don't you tell the Steinhoffers how special Audrey was and how much she will be missed?"

Pamela thought about her mother's suggestion. Admittedly it was a good idea, but she had never written a sympathy note before, and she wasn't sure she could do it.

Grabbing her school books, Pamela headed toward her bedroom. Her mother called after her, "Pamela, are you going to write the letter?"

"Maybe," Pamela said unconvincingly as she disappeared into her room.

The next day at school, all anyone could talk about was the tragic accident that had taken Audrey Steinhoffer's life.

As the day passed, the gruesome story was hashed and rehashed.

Each time it was told, the details were changed or exaggerated.

By the end of the day, so many different versions of the story had been invented, it was impossible for anyone to know exactly what had happened.

Only one fact remained unchanged. Audrey Steinhoffer was dead.

When Pamela came home from school that day, she went straight to her room. She was unloading her school books onto her bed when she noticed several sheets of light blue stationery stacked neatly on her desk.

It was the same kind of stationery Pamela's mother had used for the sympathy letter she had written to the Steinhoffers.

Pamela knew immediately that the stationery had been placed on her desk so she would remember to write a sympathy letter to the Steinhoffers.

Staring at the stationery, Pamela plopped herself into her desk chair and sighed out loud.

After a short while, Pamela began to rummage through her bottom desk drawer. Soon she found the class picture that had been taken earlier that year.

Pamela ran her finger across each row of faces until she located the one that belonged to Audrey.

For the first time, she examined the last school portrait that would be taken of Audrey Steinhoffer.

Audrey did not have a pretty face, and the fact that she wore glasses and was short and chunky didn't help.

In addition to her lack of traditional beauty, Audrey was only an average student with no apparent musical, artistic, or athletic talent.

One might easily conclude that Audrey was a person without any special qualities.

Suddenly Pamela glanced at the clock. "Oh, no," she moaned. "I'm going to be late for the club meeting!"

She quickly gathered her things together and rushed to find her mother.

"Mom, I need to go to the clubhouse," Pamela stated. "I'll be back in time to set the table for dinner."

Pamela's mother reached out and took hold of her daughter's arm. "Just a minute, Pamela," she said. "Did you have a chance to . . ." Pamela knew what her mother was going to ask and felt compelled to interrupt.

"Mom, I can't write that sympathy letter," she whined.

"Why not?" Pamela's mother questioned, and Pamela responded.

"You suggested I write about Audrey's special qualities . . . and . . . well, I don't want to sound disrespectful, but the truth is . . . Audrey didn't have any special qualities."

Pamela's remark caused her mother to challenge her. "Pamela, how can you say that? You *know* every person has special qualities. You also know that every person has a unique role in life. Audrey Steinhoffer was no exception to the rule!"

Pamela found it difficult to look into her mother's eyes, so she stared at the floor. She knew her mother was right. The fact that every human being is one of a kind was something Pamela had learned years ago.

Finally the absence of conversation became unbearable for Pamela, and she spoke up. "You're right, Mother. I'm sorry I said what I did about Audrey."

Promising her mother that she would give the sympathy letter another try, Pamela left home and ran to the clubhouse.

The Human Race Club had assembled together in the clubhouse. They had waited for Pamela to show up, but when she failed to do so, they decided to start the meeting without her.

Teddy was about to begin the meeting when Pamela burst into the clubhouse. She was out of breath and found it difficult to talk. "I'm sorry I'm late."

Because Pamela had never been late, the club members were curious about what had detained her.

Teddy asked the inevitable question. "How come you're late, Pamela?"

Pamela took a deep breath and then answered, "My mom and I were talking about Audrey Steinhoffer."

Pamela's remark began the conversation that had been waiting to happen. Considering the fact that everyone in the clubhouse knew Audrey, it would have been almost impossible for them to talk about anything else at the time.

Maggie was the first to comment, "You know, Audrey was on my softball team. She was a terrible player, but everybody really liked having her on the team. I guess it was because Audrey was always the first to compliment you when you did something good, and she was the first to encourage you when you did something bad."

"Yeah, I know what you mean," A.J. said somberly. "I remember the time our class was divided into two teams for a spelling contest, and I misspelled the word that caused my team to lose. I was really feeling awful. Then, during recess, Audrey came up to me and she said, 'A.J., you know, why don't you think about the 27 words you spelled right instead of the one word you spelled wrong?' I thought about it. And you know, she was right, and I was feeling a lot better."

Teddy nodded his head in agreement and then began to speak. "Sounds like the time I gave my speech in front of the whole student body. I worked hard to get that speech just right, and I felt as if I had done a good job. But Audrey was the only one who said anything to me. You could always count on Audrey for a compliment."

Not wanting to be left out, Casey added his story to what was being said. "Remember that bake sale we had at school? No one bought my cookies. But when Audrey found out, she bought a whole bunch of them. Now that I think back, I realize that was a pretty nice thing for her to do."

Pamela had been listening to everyone speak when all of a sudden she stood up and blurted out, "I'm sorry, you guys. I've got to go home! There's something I need to do."

Then, leaving a puzzled group of club members behind, Pamela raced home where she closed herself in her bedroom.

One hour later Pamela emerged from her room holding a letter she had written neatly on the light blue stationery.

When Pamela's mother realized what Pamela had done, she smiled. "May I read my letter to you, Mom?" Pamela shyly asked.

"Please do!" her mother said enthusiastically.

Pamela cleared her throat and began to read. "Dear Mr. and Mrs. Steinhoffer,

Audrey always said the nicest things to everyone. I never heard her say one mean thing. Any time the people around Audrey felt bad, she would do her best to make them feel better. Audrey showed my friends and me how people should treat each other. We were very lucky to know Audrey for as long as we did because she was a very special person. I will never forget the things I have learned from Audrey. Sincerely, Pamela Chin."

The lump in Pamela's mother's throat made it impossible for her to speak. But the big hug she gave Pamela said enough. Pamela had come to realize that Audrey was a special person, and in the process she had been reminded that she was special too.

So what can we learn from all of this?

When Pamela first began to evaluate Audrey, she limited her evaluation to a very few categories: looks, grades, art, and music.

This is why Pamela concluded Audrey had no special qualities. It is important to remember that there are hundreds of ways people can excel and express their uniqueness.

Discovering a person's unique qualities begins with believing the person is special.

Once Pamela acknowledged that everyone is special, she was able to explore and discover the ways in which Audrey was special.

Finding a person's special qualities can be good for the person and benefit you as well.

People are more likely to develop and use the good qualities they know about. When people express their good qualities, they contribute to the lives of everyone around them.

Finding the special qualities in other people will help you find the special qualities in yourself.

And realizing you are special will make your life more meaningful and enjoyable.

EPILOG

On the day of Audrey Steinhoffer's funeral, the school was closed so the students could attend the services. The children's choir from Audrey's church sang, and several people shared their memories of Audrey.

These things were beautiful, but almost everyone who attended the funeral agreed that the most touching part of the service was the reading of a letter.

It had been written by one of Audrey's friends on light blue stationery.

The End

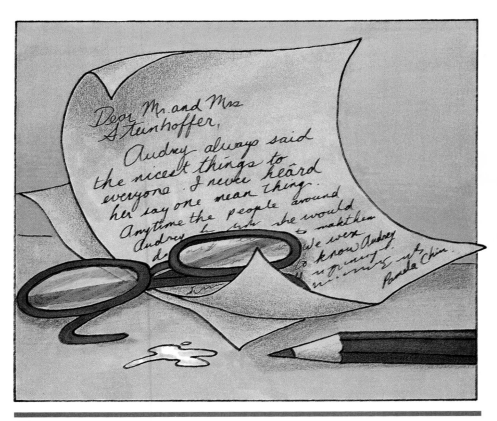